Gautam Nadkarni

Toasting The Yogi
Selected Haibun and Haiga

Olympia Publishers
London

www.olympiapublishers.com
OLYMPIA PAPERBACK EDITION

Copyright ©Gautam Nadkarni 2023

The right of Gautam Nadkarni to be identified as author of this work has been asserted in accordance with sections 77 and 78 of the Copyright, Designs and Patents Act 1988.

All Rights Reserved

No reproduction, copy or transmission of this publication
may be made without written permission.
No paragraph of this publication may be reproduced,
copied or transmitted save with the written permission of the
publisher, or in accordance with the provisions
of the Copyright Act 1956 (as amended).

Any person who commits any unauthorised act in relation to
this publication may be liable to criminal
prosecution and civil claims for damage.

A CIP catalogue record for this title is
available from the British Library.

ISBN: 978-1-80074-532-2

This is a work of fiction. Names, characters, businesses, places, events and incidents are either the products of the author's imagination or used in a fictitious manner. Any resemblance to actual persons, living or dead, or actual events is purely coincidental.

First Published in 2023

Olympia Publishers
Tallis House
2 Tallis Street
London
EC4Y 0AB
Printed in Great Britain

"Put your worry beads away! This collection of haiga and haibun by Gautam Nadkarni will make you smile, think, and fine-tune your thoughts to the foibles of living. The haiga functions as a spice for his haibun and this combining of his two signature forms work very well to lead the reader on a journey of their own making."

— Michael Rehling, founding editor of Failed Haiku Journal, USA

"Gautam Nadkarni's Toasting The Yogi, a book of haibun rooted in the Indian ethos, will provide you with many chuckles and revelations about the idiosyncrasies and tragedies of our lives. From character sketches of the narrator and his family to familiar scenes in India, this book reminds me of P. G. Wodehouse in an Indian avatar! It's not often you come across an author who has such good control of his chosen genre."

— Kala Ramesh, author of: beyond the horizon beyond, India

Dedication

This book is dedicated to my beloved siblings. Jyoti, my elder sister; Ashwin, my elder brother; and Nitin, my younger brother. Guys, you rock. You really do! Fictitious though the episodes detailed within may be, they have undoubtedly been inspired by your shenanigans. XXX

Contents

The Trade-Off	10
Pandora's Box	12
The Claus in the Contract	13
Leapfrog	15
Another School of Thought	16
The Writing on the Wall	17
Underdogs and other Breeds	19
Hard Won	20
A Wealth of Flaws	21
Beating a Retreat	24
On Edge	25
Idle Worship	26
Pipe Dreams	28
The Hole Truth	29
Rebel Without a Sauce	30
Horse Sense	32
A Close Shave with Destiny	33
The Workaholic	34
Courting Disaster	37
Mellow Drama	38
Jokes Apart	40
Ig-Nobel	42
In-Site	43
The Meek Shall Inherit the Mirth	44
Toasting the Yogi	46
Into the Drink	47
Bibliophilia and Other Ailments	48
Things Could be Verse	50

Steering Clear of Trouble	51
Hard Rock	52
The Agent of Doom	54
In Spirit	56
New Year's Peeve	57
Making Allowances	60
Checkmate	61
Cookbook for the Religious	62
Spellbound	64
Putting on Dog	65
Theory Weary	66
Ship in a Bottle	68
Awash and Dry	69
Poetic Injustice	70
Pulling up Short	73
Strait and Narrow	74
Begging Your Pardon	75
Hard to Swallow	77
Hot Couture	79
The Moon and Tuppence	81
Upliftment	82
Weekly Horror-scope	85
The Bitter Half	86
Ye Gods	88
Tree is Company	89
The Portraiture	90
Egg-ceptional	93
Issues with Paper Tissues	95
Chasing the Sandman	96
Turning on the Juice	98
Salt and Pepper	100

The Trade-Off

When I was three Mother confided in me that I would soon be a brother again. I strongly disapproved. I already had two older siblings whom I was barely able to tolerate. The very notion of one more seemed to put the lid on it. Merely because there was a huge discount sale at the baby shop did not mean one should rush about madly buying every newbie in sight. I still squirmed at the memory of my experiences with infants. The squalling brats tended to treat everyone who held them as portable loos. Just picking them up was like turning on the faucet. Therefore, it is small wonder that I disapproved. I mentioned this to Mom but she said she couldn't go back on the contract. Sheesh! The least she could've done was consulted me before parting with the cash.

   the lawyer...
   still looking for the fine print
   in the greeting card

Then one day I was taken to the maternity home to meet my brand-new brother. I examined the product closely, shook the onion and told Mother she'd got a raw deal. Where were his teeth? I asked in concern. I pointed out that we'd have to invest in a pair of dentures. And everyone knew about grandfather and his dentures. He kept misplacing them except at photo shoots.

   Finally, my new kid brother was brought home. Much to my dismay the crib which once was mine was now to be used for bro. Annoyed, I asked Mom where my cat was to sleep now. She said callously that felines could manage. I was glad Tom hadn't overheard her. He has a very sensitive disposition. Well, all of us adjusted to the new abomination. Into every life a little rain must fall. And rain is the right word, I can tell you.

   However, I made it very plain to the mater that a German shepherd pup would have been a better deal.

dog shelter
one of the canines mistakes me
for a lamp post

(Published in Drifting Sands Haibun— Issue #6 December 2020)

Pandora's Box

When I was six Father brought me a box of crayons. In twelve brilliant shades. I was thrilled. I counted all the things I could do with them on my pinkies. Mother suggested that I use them for colouring pictures. Of course, I found the idea droll. Then the mater told me to go to my room and stay out of mischief because some family friends were to visit us in the evening. Since I would be in my room for ages and ages' I decided to do some drawing and colouring.

I first drew an elephant. Coloured it pink. Did some mountains in psychedelic shades. The setting sun I coloured green. A stream running diagonally through seemed about right in a lurid shade of red. Orange clouds dotted the brown sky.

I stepped back to examine my handiwork. I added a few finishing touches and then I was through. I even signed my work with a flourish.

I imagined Dad and Mom going gaga over my painting and proudly declaring me an artist for the times. I almost felt sorry for Picasso and Salvador Dali, Stout fellows,talented too, but they had met their match in me. I was still strutting about the room cockily when Mom opened the bedroom door and peered inside. I don't think I will ever understand mothers. Really.

Instead of admiring my artwork for the masterpiece it was,she shrieked. Like a banshee who has had her toes trodden upon with spiked shoes.

Then she was scrubbing the bedroom wall vigorously with sponge and soap trying to erase my modernistic landscape, cloud by cloud, stroke by stroke. All the while muttering what she would like to do to Dad for being ass enough to arm me with a dangerous weapon like a box of crayons. I believe her plans for Father included boiling oil and a blunt skinning knife too.

    art show opens...
    the critic's three-page-review
    on the samosas served

The Claus in the Contract

When I was six I looked forward to Christmas Eve in a way that would've shamed a devout Christian. For heaven's sake, I didn't even know the meaning of Christian. Besides, what's that got to do with a roly-poly Santa Claus who went around in his sleigh dispersing gifts from an apparently bottomless gunny sack. All you needed to be was a good kid. If only for the last four days before Santa's ETA.

Going to bed on Christmas Eve was a struggle. I insisted on keeping the nursery windows open for old Father Christmas to come through. I didn't want to make things unduly difficult for an old man. But sis had other ideas. She wanted the windows shut to keep out mosquitoes. I found her most unrealistic. And even told her not to be childish.

Then Mother intervened with the information that Santa came down chimneys. When I pointed out the glaring absence of chimneys in our third-floor apartment sis pooh-poohed the idea. Finally, I went to bed disgruntled and convinced that Santa would give our home a miss on finding himself locked out.

However, in the morning, to my utter delight, the toy car of my dreams was parked beside my pillow. I don't understand why teeth have to be brushed and breakfast eaten before playing with one's sports car. But Mom insisted. I couldn't imagine anything more irrational. But one had to make allowances for cranky adults. Especially cranky adults who swung a mean punch.

For the remainder of the day I was one happy kid. Few children could be happier than one who makes a racket with impunity using his toy Lamborghini.

Finally, the day ended and I started counting the days until the next Yuletide,impatiently.

   letter to Santa...
   I ask Dad how to spell
   Kalashnikov

(Published in Failed Haiku — March 2020 issue)

TAKEAWAY COUNTER —
I LOOK AT THE PRETTY ATTENDANT
WITH INTEREST

Leapfrog

Grandmother used to read fairy tales to us as children.

I remember sis getting moon-eyed after listening to the one about *The Frog Prince*. She spent the next few hours examining every bush and looking under stones for anything remotely resembling a frog. But no luck! She almost despaired but I told her to persevere. Then she discovered a toad beneath the harrow. She wondered if it would serve the purpose. Perhaps the frog prince was in reality a toad prince. Girls in fairy tales were notoriously ignorant, she told me. I had to agree.

"Well, what's the next step?" she asked.

"You have to kiss the toad, of course," I said, pointing out the obvious.

"Yuck!" she said, grimacing. "Look at all those warts."

I had to admit that the creature in question was far from kissable. I suggested she just close her eyes tight and get it over with. She looked doubtful. I left her to her task and later asked her how things turned out.

"I did kiss the toad... but he did not turn into a prince," she complained bitterly.

I patted her on the arm and advised her to kiss every toad she came across. No telling when she might turn lucky.

She said she might spend an eternity kissing toads and grow old by the time she hit pay dirt.

"And you can't marry a prince who is young enough to be your grandson," she groaned.

That was yesterday. Today grandma read SnowWhite to us. Sis has been standing before the looking glass ever since.

Muttering, "Who's the fairest of them all?"

My heart bleeds for my sister.

    samosa stall
    ...the Maharaja flaunts
    his gold credit card

(Published in Failed Haiku — April 2020 issue)

Another School of Thought

When I was eight Dad took us all to Pune on our quarterly visit to my brother who went to boarding school in that great city. Bro had himself opted for the school under the impression that it was fun and games. And every time we visited him he went on like a martyr who was obliged to eat the ghastliest food imaginable at the hostel.

He spoke of the horrors of consuming aubergines and bell gourds on a daily basis. And the teensy-weensy portions of dessert he had to make do with. He repeatedly stressed that he had all but forgotten the meaning of ice cream. This was news to me. I couldn't imagine anyone surviving without scoops of chocolate ice cream ladled out in large bowls. He did look thin and a little pale, I noticed.

Dad took us to the neighbourhood coffee shop where bro continued complaining between mouthfuls of French fries dripping with ketchup and slurps of chilled Coca Cola. I nodded my head sympathetically as I dug into my fish and chips. I must mention at this point, that a forkful of fish when chewed along with potato chips, is heaven on earth. I was consequently in raptures as I gave a patient hearing to my brother's lurid description of what transpires when an erring lad is administered ten of the juiciest on the seat of his trousers with a cane. And all for refusing to eat his aubergine and following this up by shoving the offending vegetable down the neck of the boy on the next seat. Ten of the juiciest! Gosh! And everything I had heard about Nazi concentration camps sprang to mind. I empathised. I nodded my head solemnly. I wouldn't be surprised if I actually wiped a tear from my eyes.

Then Dad, Mom and I dropped bro at the gates of, what I had secretly labelled, 'The Dungeons' and drove back to Mumbai. Till our next visit three months hence.

    exposition
    the teacher talks at length
    on brevity

(Published in Failed Haiku — August 2018 issue)

The Writing on the Wall

When I was eight my class teacher at school summoned Mom and Dad to complain about me.

"His handwriting is terrible," she said. "I don't know what is to become of him."

When he came home, Father looked glum. As if I had just been caught flirting with the maid.

When the principal, at the parent-teacher meeting, broached the topic with the pater in that conspiratorial tone reserved for discussing felonies, the folks decided things had indeed come to a pretty pass and desperate remedies were required.

"It's no use," said the counsellor to whom I was taken. "The facts have to be faced. However sordid. Yes. I see no future for your son other than his taking up the medical profession."

Mother almost fainted and Dad was traumatised. To think that their son would spend his miserable life cutting up people and jabbing them with hypodermic syringes and other instruments of torture. It was appalling.

Word spread among friends and relatives and many came to commiserate. They told Mom and Dad to be strong. Some suggested Vedic rituals and offerings to the gods. A pall of gloom hung over our little home and everybody went about with long faces.

Finally I did go to medical school. But flunked in the entrance exam because the examiner could not make out what the deuce I'd written.

Now I am seriously contemplating other options. Like becoming a waiter at a bar. Most of the patrons are too sozzled and squiggly eyed to read what you've written.

medics' canteen...
a nurse buttering her bread
with the scalpel.

(Published in Failed Haiku — January 2020 issue)

Underdogs and other Breeds

As a boy of nine I was told by the moral science teacher at school to show compassion to underdogs. This appealed to me in a big way. I mean I always had compassion for dogs—and the more under, the more the compassion.

Upon reaching home I emptied the biscuit tin and went in search of deserving canines or underdogs. Have it your way. And the first thing I found was a dog under the flyover. Mixed breed. But then you don't need a pedigree to wolf down cream crackers. Finally, when the biscuits were gone, much to my dismay, so was the mutt. That's the problem with underdogs.

I came back home determined to show compassion to more unfortunates. But Mom caught me with my hands in the biscuit jar. And you know what moms are. Doubting Thomas'. She didn't believe a word of my elaborate explanation. Said I was fabricating the whole story. Any excuse to raid the jar.

"Underdogs, bah!" Were, I believe, her exact words.

I wondered what the Moral Science teacher had to say on the subject of suspicious moms.

> kennel club---
> the uncertain pedigree
> of a hotdog

(Published in Failed Haiku — December 2018 issue)

Hard Won

When I was a lad of ten I would come home from school and immerse myself in books. Enid Blyton, Agatha Christie and P.G Wodehouse were to me as delightful and necessary as cornflakes and omelettes at breakfast. I thrived on them. But the adults were very much concerned.

"He doesn't have any playmates," complained Mother to no one in particular.

"All he does is read," said Father, with a frown. There was a general consensus that things had come to a pretty pass and couldn't possibly get worse. Then Dad came across a volume at a sidewalk stall and got a brainwave. The book was, *How To Win Friends And Influence People by Dale Carnegie.* The pater decided to fight fire with fire. And that's how the paperback came into my hands.

Well, I decided that I'd read the book carefully and win dozens of buddies just like that. So, I studied the volume word by word, chapter by chapter, and even memorised several passages. And a few days later I was ready to apply myself to winning friends and influencing people.

At close of the first day I was richer by three new friends. Dad and Mom were thrilled. They congratulated each other on money well spent and even turned mental cartwheels. Having won the friends the next part was to influence them. So, I got down to it.

Two days later, when Mother and Father came home from an outing, they were aghast to see me and my three new buddies sitting hunched up in the living room reading diligently.

I explained to Mom later. Winning the friends was the easier part. Influencing them was tougher than you'd imagine. But I'd worked hard at it, and they had ultimately seen things my way.

All four of us had since become members of the local circulating library.

   pin-drop silence...
   the librarian seeking in vain
   whom she may shush

(Published in Failed Haiku — June 2020 issue)

A Wealth of Flaws

When I was in the fifth grade the class teacher summoned my parents to tattle on me. I had seen it coming.

When Dad and Mom turned up to meet the gorgon I was called out of class. To witness my humiliation.

First Miss D'Souza criticised me for my performance in math and science. My objection that I was never cut out to be a mathematician or a scientist fell on deaf ears. Geography was another weak point with me, she said. I told her I was no explorer and seldom travelled further than to the refrigerator from the living room. Again, she played the biblical deaf adder.

Not content with the damage she'd done already, Medusa went on to ridicule my Hindi. Here I felt obliged to mention that the only Hindi I needed to know was the kind spoken in Bollywood films. For some strange reason this made the old witch raise an eyebrow. It's pretty tough to raise just one, I can tell you. I know because I've spent hours before the mirror practising.

"It's no use," said the gorgon. "I can only predict a bleak future for your son. He is going to end up as a lowly business tycoon."

She went on, "I'm sorry but you have to face the sordid facts. He may one day have billions to his name but what's the use, I ask you, if he doesn't know where Timbuktu is. He will, of course, have private yachts and personal jet planes in which to travel but imagine the humiliation in not knowing what makes a pressure cooker tick."

Father groaned and Mom clutched at her brow. But the grim soothsayer droned on mercilessly.

"Your son will undoubtedly have several mansions and a fleet of limousines but if he doesn't know the square root of pi and Pythagoras' theorem of what use is all his wealth?"

I think Dad had enough by then to give him a month of sleepless nights and Mom was sorely in need of a shoulder to weep on. They took their leave looking appropriately glum.

When I went back to class, I whispered to my buddy, Rajesh, that my horoscope looked pretty bad. Apparently, I would spend the rest of my life counting the billions I had in Swiss accounts and in the Cayman Islands.

Well, at least I knew where that was. Thank heavens!

marathon...
the globetrotter complains
of calluses

(Published in Contemporary Haibun Online — December 2020 issue)

Beating a Retreat

Ever since I was so high I had been listening to the Beatles. It came as a surprise to me therefore that they were human. I mean only a god could sing, *Desmond has a barrow in the marketplace...* But the fat kid on the second floor was adamant. They were definitely flesh and blood. I could have killed him.

Everybody emulates their God and I was no exception. What Dad objected to was my emulating him in such a loud and off-key voice, while taking a shower. But then he never had an ear for music.

Uncle bought me Beatles shoes and assorted other Beatles things. But I stopped there. I had an uneasy feeling that a Beatles haircut wouldn't be a huge success at school. Father Percy was such a prude.

second coming...
the bald man lets his hair down
at the discotheque

(Published in Contemporary Haibun Online — July 2018 issue)

On Edge

It must have been ten in the morning on a Sunday when the show started. My kid brother and I had a balcony seat. That's because the free-for-all was taking place in the house opposite ours.

The neighbours spoke a tongue which we did not understand but the gestures and raised voices told us plenty. It all began when the mother asked her offspring whose turn it was to wash the dishes. This triggered off an altercation between brother and sister which, though it started on a low-key, soon escalated into a full-fledged battle replete with the most colourful words. The mother and father soon joined the fray and though I had my bets on the patriarch it was the mater who turned out the hot favourite.

How we rooted for our respective heroes. All in all it was a wonderful show which beat freestyle wrestling any day because everyone knows that the latter is rigged. But this was the real McCoy.

We waited with bated breath for the clincher. Agog was what we were. We could scarcely guess who would succumb and who would live to tell the tale. It was a genuine edge-of-the-seat performance.

Finally, the judge's gavel came down hard. The brother was declared official dishwasher for the day and slunk away into the undergrowth. Defeated.

The grand finale was over but I had to drag my kid brother away from the veranda still shrieking for an encore. I could now understand how the gladiators drew such a crowd in ancient Rome.

    truth prevails—
    under the powdered wig
    the judge quite bald

(Published in Prune Juice — July 2019 issue)

Idle Worship

When I was a lad of thirteen, I came over all religious.

Just as I had seen Mom and Dad do I put up pictures of gods and goddesses on the walls of my room. I garlanded them with strings of marigold, burned incense sticks and knelt down every night to pray to them. And everything was hunky-dory until one morning sis invaded the sanctity of my room in her search for a missing hairclip.

I had just waved a lighted oil lamp before the gods and was deep in prayer when my sister's high-pitched voice asked me what the hell I was up to. I almost jumped out of my epidermis and looked at her reproachfully. She brushed aside the reproachful look much as one would an errant hair that tickles the nose.

"What are these posters doing here?" asked sis. "Are you crazy?"

"Atheists like you will never understand the religious mind," I told her rather pompously.

"Religious forsooth!" she said. "What's so religious about pictures of Clint Eastwood, Marlon Brando, Audrey Hepburn and..." she paused to identify the fourth. "And Shirley MacLaine?"

"Pooh!" I chided. "What would an agnostic know about gods! They have to be seen to be believed. Have you seen Clint Eastwood in *Dirty Harry,* Audrey Hepburn in *Roman Holiday?"* I asked bitterly.

Sis rolled her eyes heavenward. Then set upon the task of systematically ripping off the posters from the walls. I wept copiously of course. I even contemplated wailing and beating my breast. But religion does not die so easily.

Now, decades later, I have real gods and goddesses mounted on my walls: Usain Bolt, Rafael Nadal and Serena Williams.

confessional—
the priest wears a cassock
and a smirk

(Published in Failed Haiku — May 2019 issue)

Pipe Dreams

Ever since I was thirteen I have always been an avid reader of *Sherlock Holmes* stories. The brainchild of Sir Arthur Conan Doyle. And I always dreamt of becoming a great detective like him.

I dissected and studied his methods in teensy weensy detail. Just as he always bade Dr Watson to do. And analysed his deductions thoroughly leaving no stone unturned. His logic I was convinced would have made philosophers and mathematicians sit up and take notice. And more than ever I was positive that the reason his brain worked like a well-oiled piece of machinery was because of the pipe he smoked.

Now it so transpired that Father smoked a pipe too. In fact, he had a large collection of briar pipes that would have made Sherlock Holmes green with envy. I have often wondered why Dad chose to be a businessman rather than a private eye. After all, he had what it takes to be the world's greatest sleuth, his pipe collection.

One afternoon when the pater was taking a snooze I snuck into his room and clandestinely extracted a pipe from his box. Also, his tobacco pouch and a three-pronged steel instrument to tamp down the tobacco. After which I tiptoed out and made my way to the terrace. I stuffed the weed into the bowl just as I'd seen Father do and lit up. So far so good. Next, I inhaled deeply of the smoke… The next few minutes are extremely hazy but what I do recall is that my lungs appeared to have caught fire and the entire chest heaved in an attempt to come out through my mouth. Several minutes later, although my chest had changed its mind about exiting my body my throat was parched and burning.

And at that moment I took a decision that was to change my life forever and ever. Yessir! I resolved never to become a detective.

Scotland Yard…
wondering how they got along
without whodunnits

(Published in Failed Haiku — August 2020 issue)

The Hole Truth

When Apollo 11 landed on the moon in July 1969 and Neil Armstrong stepped gingerly onto the lunar surface, all set to take a giant step for mankind, I was in the ninth grade at school. Naturally, like the rest of the kids, I was agog with excitement. So, I grilled Father over breakfast.

I asked Dad rather apprehensively whether the theory about the moon being made of green cheese still held. He lowered the newspaper he was reading and shook his head regretfully. I was disappointed.

"How about blue cheese," I said.

He checked the papers again and replied in the negative. I wasn't convinced. I was quite sure that the man on the moon had questionable scruples. He was obviously trying to get the best price for himself. But I stuck doggedly on and went through the whole gamut of cheeses, both processed and uncooked. But the answer was always, no. So finally, like a true scientist, I grudgingly accepted the verdict that whatever else may be in, cheese was definitely out. Apparently, the theory, like Swiss cheese, was full of holes.

Now I am working on a new theory after collating all the facts gleaned from the discoveries made. This time I am convinced that I just cannot go wrong. I am working hard on the thesis that the only natural satellite of the earth is made of marshmallow. Everything checks out beautifully.

All I have to do now is figure out the flavour.

plump moon...
ransacking the shelves for
sugar-free candyfloss

(Published in Narrow Road — August 2020 issue)

Rebel Without a Sauce

Dear Dad,

I don't know what could have prompted me to volunteer to attend this boarding school. I must have been drunk at the time.

It's not as though I was demanding sirloin steak every day with one of those rare vintage wines that make you feel like heaven. But c'mon, Dad. Not even on the weekends? Have a heart. And the beaks here put the Gestapo to shame. Always insisting that we put in three hours a day on the homework. Imagine swotting like my life depends on it when I could be doing fun things like backing gee-gees and getting high on smack. It's a crime.

The other day I appeared for the math test and fared badly. I never heard the end of it. They asked the most ridiculous questions. If a quintal of aubergines cost so-and-so rupees, how much would you have to pay for a cruise on the Nile? The answer is obvious but my pocket calculator conked out just then. Too bad! Now they won't get a paisa for the cruise or for the aubergines.

I believe they even censor the letters we write home. Dad, stay warned. If you don't receive this letter at all, you can safely assume that the headmaster and his fellow Mafiosi have deposited me at the bottom of the ocean in a concrete kimono. I have been noticing the gleam in their eyes for quite a while.

Well, I have to go now. It's dinnertime, and a guy has to eat. Even if it tastes like last year's garbage. Give my love to mum. And spare her these gruesome details. She always had a weak stomach.

With much affection,
Your quietly suffering son,
Dippy

red wine—
undecided on the vintage
of the steak

(Published in Failed Haiku — February 2019 issue)

Horse Sense

I was never a believer in fortune tellers. At least not until my sister consulted an astrologer who told her confidently that she would marry a prince who would ride off with her on his white steed into the sunset.

How could one believe in such nonsense in this enlightened age of space travel? I was positive he meant a white SUV and I said so. But sis was adamant. She said the steed could be a retired polo pony. There were plenty of them around. I had to admit this made sense. I remembered my trip to a hill station where the horse that threw me turned out to be a polo pony. And I had to pay the horse owner for my troubles.

But, I said, where would he find a sunset to ride into? Mumbai being a coastal city he would have to swim off into the sunset. Dashed sticky it could get, I warned her. A guy can hardly stay afloat with wet clothes clinging to him.

Sis looked triumphant as she made a counterargument. Rather like the prosecutor in court asking the defendant where he was between 9 p.m. and 9.10 p.m. on the night of the gruesome murder. Maybe the prince would be clad in swimming trunks, she said. I told her she would always have to go around in a full bathing costume. No telling when and where her Prince Charming would pop out of the bushes riding his polo pony. One had to be prepared for all contingencies. The point registered.

Now sis is going to consult the soothsayer before buying another bathing costume. I certainly hope her prince isn't colourblind.

Derby results…
the jockey still complaining
of sore buttocks

(Published in Drifting Sands Haibun— April 2020 issue)

A Close Shave with Destiny

I received my very first electric shaver from Dad shortly after graduating from high school. Till then I had contented myself with a trimmer. It was a big day for me, of course. I was now what I had always dreamt of being since babyhood. A Grown-Up.

After my first shave with the machine I strutted about importantly hoping people would notice my clean jowls. At least smell the aftershave. But not a single look of admiration came my way. I found this most annoying. I mean what's the point of standing in front of a mirror for hours and shaving off one's fuzz if ultimately nobody is going to notice it. I had to concede that what I had always suspected was true. People were barbarians. Beneath the thin veneer of civilisation every single person was a savage. I wouldn't have been surprised if the entire lot hadn't tied me to a stake with thongs and danced around me, singing lustily.

The girl next door was the next guinea pig. I had always admired her large, brown eyes and the way she fluttered her long lashes at me. I went onto the veranda and was prepared to wait indefinitely when, as if on cue, she came onto hers. When I greeted her with a "Hi!" she looked mystified. Didn't seem to recognise me. When I introduced myself to the object of my dreams she burst out laughing. A tinkling laugh but this time it jarred. She felt it was her duty to explain that without the face fuzz I looked like one of those trans—something. I felt like dashing to my room, burying my face in the pillow and weeping copiously.

I decided after the pillow was soaking wet that I would retire to a dark, lonely cave in the Himalayas and become a hermit. One with a long unkempt beard that swept the ground.

Khajuraho
the contortionist picks up
a trick or two

(Published in Narrow Road —2018)

The Workaholic

When I finally graduated from university Father decided I had spent enough time on tomfoolery and it was high time I entered the family business. I decided to prepare myself for the ordeal ahead and went and bought myself a pair of grey pinstriped trousers, a white shirt and a nice, black necktie. I also purchased a Samsonite briefcase to look 'the part'. It's no use entering the world of commerce without looking like a minor potentate.

And then the big day came, my first day at the office.

After making sure my clothes were well pressed I pulled them on and spent a half-hour adjusting my tie to get the perfect knot. These things count. I'm certain Richard Branson would never have amassed his billions if he hadn't got his necktie knotted right. Wearing my Italian leather shoes I followed Father and my brothers downstairs and got into the car after fussing about with the crease on my trouser legs.

At the office building I rode up to the third floor on an ancient elevator and entered the office with a confident stride. All the staff were on their feet wishing us good morning which I acknowledged with a courteous nod. It was only after the cabin door was closed that I let go of my breath, which I had been holding all along, and a shirt button gave. Desperate, I hunted in vain for a safety pin but finally settled for a paper clip to fasten my shirt front. I almost despaired because I was positive, I would be the laughing stock of the business community. Still, we magnates are made of sterner stuff than you'd imagine.

I soon got down to office work which began with my raising the swivel chair by a notch or two so that I wouldn't bang my chin on the tabletop. I then leaned back in my chair, taking care that it didn't topple over backwards. Putting my fingertips together, like I'd seen on television, I plotted in tiny detail how I would spend the vast fortune I was about to make.

And suddenly it was lunchtime.

I decided to partake of a quick meal in the office itself and had a luncheon delivered to my cabin—only four courses, mind. I tucked the napkin into my shirt collar and, picking up the cutlery, got right down to it. With the luncheon consumed I gave a dainty belch, put up my feet, and realised for the hundredth time why Spaniards insisted on a siesta after the midday fiesta. That's what makes Spain so great.

Upon waking up I felt refreshed enough to tackle huge business deals and negotiate like the dickens. This reminded me that I had yet to go through the office files and study them in great detail so I could take grand decisions, momentous decisions.

I began by deciding that there was no time for it like the morrow.

leisure reading...
the tycoon reaches for
his passbook

(Published in Contemporary Haibun Online — April 2021 issue)

Courting Disaster

I have to modestly admit that in my college days I was known as a dashing young fellow. That's right. I was always dashing to the canteen on the campus. Sometimes to savour their heavenly potato chips. And sometimes to wolf down a cheeseburger or two when I had the bread and the inclination. So, it came as no surprise to my buddies when Bela, the class beauty, made passes at me.

She asked me to accompany her to a Chinese restaurant at Colaba Causeway known for its dumplings. Of course, I wasn't fool enough to pass up such a golden opportunity. I mean, the dumplings there are out of this world. I was already drooling.

On the following Saturday evening I turned up for the date. Suitably attired in a filthy sweatshirt and torn jeans. One has to keep up certain standards after all. Bela was all dolled up in an evening dress with a string of pearls around her long, slender neck. And fancy earrings.

There was some misunderstanding at the restaurant entrance when the security guard almost shooed me away mistaking me for a tramp. Well, the matter was soon sorted out and afterwards Bela and I had a hearty chuckle over it.

At dinner, when the dumplings were served, I came over all romantic and moon-eyed as I tucked into the main course and told Bela her eyes were so like the oysters I relished as a boy and how her perfume reminded me of dried shrimp. For some strange reason Bela cut up rusty. I'll never understand why. Some people are so unromantic. She marched out and left me to pay the tab.

I was nursing a black eye for days afterwards.

street food...
the chef recommends
an antidote

Mellow Drama

When my friend Rajesh caught me in a corner at a party and whispered something hoarsely to me I told him to speak up.

"For heaven's sake!" he said, shushing me with gestures of his rather large hands. "This is private and confidential."

I rolled my eyes skyward for I knew what was coming.

"I say, how does one go about proposing to a girl?" he asked. "I've spent sleepless nights thinking of ways but it's no use."

When I suggested getting down on one knee, holding her hand and asking her to be his, he dismissed it with a snort. He said it had to be original. Perhaps even unique. The girl in question was a novelist, he said. Always on the lookout for new plots. With a revulsion for anything in the nature of a cliche.

I pondered on it for a whole minute before I spoke. I asked him whether he could sing. If he could, I recommended bursting into song and laying bare his heart. It was fool proof, I said. Always worked in the movies. Even before the lyric was over, she would fall all over him. But he shook his head after mulling it over. No, he couldn't sing. The last time he sang in the bath his mother thought somebody had had a frightful accident and was screaming in agony. Pretty peeved she had been when he appeared before her, unscathed. So, I let that drop. Although I still thought it a sound idea.

Then I suggested reading out a soliloquy from *Romeo and Juliet*. That should impress her. He would have her eating out of his hands. All he had to do was memorise part of the famous balcony scene dialogue. But I cautioned him to concentrate on Romeo's words and give Juliet's a miss. Otherwise there could be complications. He said he'd do his best and departed on his mission. The next I heard from him was when he came over to present me with a wedding invitation card.

So, I finally found my true calling in life. I have set up shop as a counsellor on affairs of the heart. And let me tell you I make more money than a cardiac surgeon. All you need is a good imagination and a head planted firmly on your shoulder.

The last client, for instance, proposed marriage to his girl at a funeral parlour, just as I suggested. Now the couple are simply dying to get married.

    theatre...
    the director says my sneeze
    is not in the script.

Jokes Apart

In my final year of college all my classmates, the ambitious ones among them at least, were moon-eyed about their future careers.

One of my pals spoke devoutly about becoming a world-famous heart surgeon while another fantasised about becoming a business tycoon with a private plane and a fleet of Rolls-Royces. Yet another wished to take up law. Maybe even become a supreme court judge, eventually. When it was my turn to talk I hesitated and then told them shyly that I wanted to be a humourist.

At first they were flabbergasted. Then alarmed. They exchanged worried looks. Then someone suggested a good therapist.

"Don't worry," they said comfortingly, "he'll fix you up in a jiffy. A few electric shocks and meds will set things right. You'll be as good as new."

Another chappie, the more religious of the lot, prescribed a peace offering to the gods to the chant of certain mantras which would right the wrongs perpetuated by the position of Saturn in a certain house. He even studied my right palm intently and shook his onion sadly at first. Then he cheered up and pointed excitedly to my lifeline and the Mount of Luna and said all would be well. Nothing to fret about. All I had to do was break a few coconuts and feed a few Brahmins.

However, I was adamant. And stubborn, as few mules could dream of being. I told the congregation intensely that ever since I'd read Mark Twain in my childhood and, more recently, Groucho Marx, I had always entertained ambitions of becoming a humourist.

For some obscure reason this had them grinning hugely and a wag dismissed me as being tight as an owl. Mark Twain, indeed! Groucho Marx, hah! Someone even asked me whether I'd been having a few behind their backs and there were loud guffaws and much slapping of thighs.

And I hadn't even cracked a joke yet.

> house full...
> the new stand-up comedian
> lays an egg

(Published in World Haiku Review — August 2020 issue)

Ig-Nobel

I don't think I will ever understand sisters. Take mine for instance. Batty to the core. The epitome of superstition despite having a brother with a scientific temperament. A brother, in fact, who is likely to win a Nobel Prize and whose name will be uttered one day in hushed tones, in much the same way a tippler would utter the words Veuve Clicquot.

When I mentioned this to sis she immediately held out a lucky talisman. She said if I hung it around my neck, like a dog's collar, I would certainly get the Nobel. I laughed till the tears streamed down my cheeks. Or at least I would have if she didn't have that dangerous gleam in her eyes. She excused herself and came back from her room with a scrap of paper. Said if I chanted the mantra written on it a hundred times a day my success was guaranteed. She also advised me never to get up in the morning from the left side of my bed. It would be disastrous, she warned. I told her not to be ridiculous. We scientists scoff at superstition, I told her grandly. I pooh-poohed the idea.

The following morning, when I was brushing my teeth, my forehead suddenly turned clammy with sweat and I fell into a blue funk. Try as I might, I could not recall which side of the bed I had gotten out of.

Now I'm wondering about that Nobel...

Friday the 13th...
the black cat crossing my path
gets run over

(Published in Contemporary Haibun Online — April 2020 issue)

In-Site

I was only thirty-five when I got into real estate. Well, at least sort of...

The building complex was coming up in Thane, a suburb of Mumbai, and I was entrusted with the mission of showing prospective clients around the site. That is, when I wasn't relaxing with a soft drink whacked from the fridge in the common room and a cigarette.

It was when I was on the third Coke and the fifth cigarette that the supervisor bloke blew in, eyeballed me and raised a brow. Naturally, I bristled. I can take a hint as well as the next person and I got right down to earning my slave wages. After all, I wasn't the type to goof off.

Having worked very hard showing the flats to an old fuddy-duddy who looked like he had wandered in to ask for directions to the supermarket and practically wearing myself down to skin and bones I was back in the common room quaffing a well-earned can of Coke and a ciggy in the space of five whole minutes. Though it did seem like an eternity.

When the supervisor walked in I expected nothing short of appreciation and a pat on the back. Also, a brief emotional speech interspersed with sobs on how they could never have managed without me. I will never understand, therefore, why the gentleman tore his hair and sputtered out my marching orders.

All the way home in the train I was pondering on what a strange world this is.

apartment building
...whistling as I park my bike
by the neighbour's Rolls

(Published in Ephemerae — July 2018 issue)

The Meek Shall Inherit the Mirth

Some people excel at making cracks and some are eternal scapegoats. There appears to be a general consensus that I fall into the latter category.

It is a common sight, me grinning sheepishly as some devilishly clever fellow makes all the witty remarks and steals the thunder. I bring out the worst in people, or the best depending on whose side you're on. As you can well imagine it makes me very popular with wiseacres who are always on the lookout for punching bags. I once thought that a wiseacre was an excellent investment in real estate. Silly me! I guess that was never my area of expertise.

Parties are places where wits abound. Perhaps it has something to do with the spirit of the occasion. Particularly the type which comes in bottles. Once under the influence of a single malt I dared to try my hand at sarcasm. Or so I was told when I was sufficiently sober. I couldn't believe my ears. The victim of my razor-sharp tongue apparently couldn't believe his either. Suffice it to say that whatever I did say to him, this bloke has been avoiding eye contact with me ever since.

    psychology class...
    the sedating effect
    of a lecture

(Published in Under The Basho — 2018)

KRSNA DEVOTEEooo
STILL STRUGGLING TO PRONOUNCE
THE NAME.

Toasting the Yogi

There is much to be said in favour of austerity. I said as much to my companion who sat beside me in the Dreamliner as we flew to Tokyo. I quoted Swami Vivekananda to him between sips of champagne and we agreed on the principle of meditation and clarity of vision as I ordered another glass of Veuve Clicquot. I pointed out the benefits of vegetarianism as I chewed on sirloin steak done medium-rare. And finally, I remember advocating awareness before I nodded off to sleep.

   pub chatter...
   worried about his hippie son
   smoking cigarettes

(Published in Cattails — April 2018 issue)

Into the Drink

I once attended a cocktail party. No, wait! Don't sound the trumpets yet. Actually I was visiting an old college friend and dropped in unannounced. The blister had thrown open his house and bar to a drove of thirsty journalists and was in the middle of his fourth scotch when I knocked. Of course, he was glad to see me and insisted on my staying on. He could have been a little more discreet, however.

"Oh, it's you!" he said thickly. "It's about time."

Glad to see me, as I said earlier. Then he looked at me closely through the haze and blinked twice.

"Good God! I thought it was the help." He looked disappointed. "Very well," he continued, "Now that you're here make yourself useful."

And that's how I ended up serving the whiskies and pink gins at the do.

Halfway through the evening I spotted my old crèche nanny standing by herself. We chatted animatedly about the good old days for fifteen minutes before I realised, she was someone else. I must say I frowned on fate overdoing things a bit. It was becoming a habit. Events are a little foggy after that but I am told that after the dust had settled I staggered home in the wee hours singing a ribald old ditty.

packed tavern...
the bartender pouring out
tales of woe

(Published in Failed Haiku—April 2018 issue)

Bibliophilia and Other Ailments

I always loved bookkeeping. As an activity. I would borrow books from others and keep them. On my little bookshelf. Neatly lined.

I remember first borrowing the Bhagavad Gita from a friend. A translation in English, of course. I wasn't foolish enough to borrow one in Sanskrit. It would have made an obscure work even more obscure. Then another pal bought himself a book on Relativity. I was intrigued. I have plenty of relatives, you know. They keep crawling out from the woodworks. I can't stand them. If they are not borrowing money from you they are borrowing books. It's the latter type that cheese me off. And so, I borrowed the Relativity volume from the aforementioned friend. It now occupies pride of place on my small bookrack.

A visitor once asked me if I had read all the books on my shelves. I was shocked to the core and told him so. Whoever heard of reading books! I'm not stupid, you know.

   time is relative...
   my boss still shouts at me
   for coming late

(Published in Failed Haiku—2018 issue)

KENNEL CLUB—
THE UNCERTAIN PEDIGREE
OF A HOTDOG

Things Could be Verse

When I was invited to read out my poems at the literary event in Pune City I was more overwrought than a cat that has sauntered casually onto a hot tin roof. I mean, consider the situation. I had to read out my verse to a discerning audience and I didn't have a thing to wear.

My brother suggested a green polo-neck T-shirt with a tan-coloured jacket and matching trousers. An excellent idea, I had to concede, but I had none of these things in my wardrobe. So, I went shopping in the mall at Lower Parel.

It was in the third store that I found a polo-neck tee of exactly the desired shade. Next on the agenda were the jacket and trousers. This proved a little more difficult. I had to visit half a dozen retail outlets before I hit pay dirt. I tried them on and danced a few steps before a mirror in the changing room till I was thoroughly convinced it couldn't be better. I was confident I would have the audience eating out of my hands. Flushed with thoughts of victory I came home.

At last, when D-Day dawned, I got up singing like a lark which has everything going for it. I wore my prized polo-neck tee shirt and the tan jacket and trouser combo and a few hours later I strode confidently into the hall where the event was to be held. Cocky as hell.

After the lesser poets had gone through their routine it was my turn. I stepped gracefully onto the stage, bowed dramatically to the crowd and reached into my coat pocket for the poems to be read out. It was then that the awful truth hit me.

I knew I had forgotten something.

> memory lapse...
> the doctor carefully takes
> his fees in advance

(Unpublished piece)

Steering Clear of Trouble

It was not so long ago that I was bitten by the driving bug. Yes, I wanted to learn to drive. What if I ever became a multimillionaire with a fleet of limousines and sports cars. Pretty silly I would look if I couldn't drive. A Maserati is not a Maserati unless you handle the baby yourself. That's what I had heard. So, there I was straining at the leash and panting for a car. Bro, ever the practical man about town, suggested I join a driving school. You have to hand it to him. It would never have occurred to me. So, I wore my best jeans and tees and joined the nearest school.

The driving instructor turned out a taciturn bloke who spoke to me in sign language all his own. But I got the drift. One was supposed to press the brake with one foot and the accelerator with the other. Or something along those lines. And off we went.

However, when the car got moving and vehicles all around started hooting their horns, I panicked. I forgot the pep talk I had received of grit and determination and all the rest and could think of only one course of action. Abandoning the whole operation and running home to mama. And that was precisely what I did do.

Days later when I had gotten over the panic symptoms with nobody the wiser I dismissed the whole sorry episode with a grunt. I told my brother that it was below the dignity of a future multimillionaire to drive his own car.

Whoever heard of Richard Branson flying his own jets.

main street—
the nonconformist drives
on the wrong side

(Published in Contemporary Haibun Online — October 2018 issue)

Hard Rock

I had always wanted a pet. Ever since I could remember. I sat down and made an elaborate list of the usual pets, people adopt and struck them out faster than I wrote them. Cats, dogs, rabbits and guinea pigs were all so passé. Then somebody suggested a rock. It struck home. The idea slowly hardened into conviction.

I made my way to an adoption centre specialising in rocks. First, a committee of three people grilled me for an hour to make sure I'd be the ideal parent for one of their loved and cherished rocks. I filled up a dozen forms and the deed was done, the pact signed.

Back home, Mom insisted on calling a Brahmin priest over to chant appropriate mantras and wave a lighted oil lamp to sanctify the entry of a new member into the family. She even broke a coconut.

Came the naming ceremony. Everyone was full of suggestions. Each worse than the other. Until I finally selected the name, Peter. The family was aghast. They had all wanted the pet named after the gods of the Hindu pantheon and here I was naming it after Peter Pan. Then bro googled the name and found it came from the root word 'petro', which meant rock.

How the family fussed over the new member. Then sis suggested feeding it. But apparently Peter was not hungry at all. He didn't take even a bite of the goodies offered.

Peter turned out an ideal pet. No long walks, no whining and scratching, no barking and howling, and no dirtying the carpet. But although we doted on him Dad felt he was much too quiet. This had us worried and we did contemplate a visit to a psychologist for counselling.

This was over a year ago. Now Peter keeps company with fellow rocks. We donated him to a kind couple who cultivate and maintain a rock garden. Peter must be very happy there.

He certainly hasn't complained as yet.

bunny rabbits…
this overwhelming need
for sex education

(Published in Failed Haiku — January 2019 issue)

EARLY BIRD...
STILL TRYING MY DARNDEST
TO TURN OFF THE ALARM

The Agent of Doom

When the doorbell rang one afternoon I tied up the dog which was snarling and straining at the leash and opened the door. Just a crack.

"Hullo!" said a cheery voice through the gap. "Hullo, hullo, hullo!"

"Are you a salesman?" I asked. Bingo has a nose for salesmen.

"Not at all, not at all!" said the alpine echo. "I bring glad tidings."

On hearing these words I yanked open the door and almost laid out the red carpet for the spectral voice. The fact was I had bought a lottery ticket with a number ending in three, as advised by the friendly neighbourhood numerologist. I was positive the ticket had been drawn and I was in for more money than you could compute on a pocket calculator.

> billing time—
> the computer salesman
> counts on his pinkies

As the door opened the voice assumed a body with a bespectacled face attached at the top. This face wore a grin that almost matched my own. After all, it isn't every day one wins the lottery. The grinning apparition came in and plonked onto the most comfortable armchair without so much as a 'by your leave'. But I didn't care. I was too busy planning how to spend the swag.

With the briefest of pauses I dashed into the kitchen and dashed back with a steaming, hot cup of tea and chocolate cream biscuits. I almost apologised to the man for not having chilled champagne handy. He ate the biscuits methodically, no doubt chewing each mouthful a hundred times as advocated by medics. Splendid fellows, medics. Having gone through the biscuits, he paused only to smile beatifically at me before slurping the tea. He then put down the plate with the air of one about to spring a cheque on me. I waited with bated breath. At last, he opened a briefcase and pulled out an envelope.

"Congratulations!" he said, beaming. "Your life insurance policy for ten thousand rupees has matured. We are sure you will want to renew the policy with us. We assure you of our best services at all times."

And with those words he slid the envelope between my numb fingers and vanished. Like a ghost at daybreak.

What could I say? I was glad I hadn't invested in a bottle of Veuve Clicquot.

celebrations—
after the champagne party,
we go for a drink

(Published in The Other Bunny — 2019)

In Spirit

It was the morning after the New Year's bash. I was nursing a massive hangover and a bottle of Veuve Clicquot when, suddenly, there was a puff of smoke which had me gagging and rubbing my eyes. A gentle cough made me glance upward and there before me stood a roly-poly gentleman in a tuxedo. The jacket a bit tight around the midriff.

"Who?" I asked the tuxedoed fellow, "Are you?" convinced it was an illusion.

"The genie of the champagne bottle, sir," said the stout illusion.

"But," I pointed out after a moment of thought, "Genies reside in brass lamps."

"Oh," laughed the apparition. "That is so passé. We genies moved into more comfortable quarters. Brass lamps can be very restrictive. However," he went on, "as is customary with us genies, may I inform you of your rights. You have but one wish to make. And I assure you I will try my best to fulfil it. But of course, there are terms and conditions."

And he conjured up a pamphlet and handed it over.

"But," I objected, "genies are supposed to grant three wishes."

"Not any more," said the genie. "At the last Genies' Convention at Geneva we decided to hone it down to one."

I figured this was too good an opportunity to miss and whipping out a sheet of paper and a ballpoint pen I made a list of things I always wanted. However, to every wish I put forth the genie had objections. A million-dollar yacht, for instance, would not fit anywhere in the seas around Mumbai. A fleet of limousines would consume oceans of petrol and run up big bills. A massive mansion would be much too impractical for a single person like me.

Whatever else he might produce, this genie was extremely adept at producing excuses. So finally, I asked for the only thing possible and practical. I asked the genie to replace the bottle of champagne he had taken up as residence.

At least I could get drunk.

formals party
…still wondering who
is the butler

(Published in The Other Bunny — 2019)

New Year's Peeve

I love New Year's Eve parties. I always have loved them. It's great to make the most daring resolutions with not the slightest intention of keeping them. And the camaraderie of friends you had all but forgotten till that moment.

It was accordingly with great enthusiasm that I invited my buddies, Dinesh and Rajesh, for a bash at my pad on the evening of thirty-first December.

Dinesh was the first to arrive. The moment he stepped in he looked around. Wild-eyed.

"Where's the booze?" he demanded.

That's what I like about him. No beating about the bush.

"Chilled lager. It's in the Frigidaire," I said with a chuckle.

"Are you crazy?" he said. "This is not a children's do."

This intrigued me.

"Did you drink as a toddler? Well, well and well. Talk about starting early," I said in surprise.

Dinu disdained to reply. Instead, he picked up his cellphone and rang up the Shri Krishna Wine Shop. He ordered several bottles of liquor I hadn't even heard of. And he uttered the names with devotion. Like mantras. Very appropriate, I recall commenting.

The doorbell rang and Rajesh entered with more bottles of elixir in his arms. I quickly sized up the situation.

"Guys," I said. "We have enough here to make a battalion drunk."

"Good," said Dinesh. "What are we waiting for!"

"There's still time for the new year," I protested.

"No time like the present," said Rajesh. "A famous sage once said, always live in the present. His name escapes me. Quite a tongue twister it is."

Finally, the new year tottered in and the old year tottered out. Or at least that's what must have happened. I wouldn't know because the three of us were too preoccupied singing ribald ditties lustily until the wee hours. After which things are a bit hazy.

I have reason to believe we had a great time.

New Year's Eve...
shouts of happy Diwali
after the fourth drink

(Published in Failed Haiku — February 2020 issue)

Making Allowances

When I scored high in Mensa I could hardly keep out the swagger from my gait. Naturally, I looked askance at those who were merely brilliant.

Well, actually, to keep the record straight, the Mensa test appeared in a popular Indian glossy somewhere between the political column on page two and the agony aunt column on page four. But I solved the whole paper all by myself. Yes sir! Though I admit to occasionally peeking at the answers given upside down on the last page. But that was to see if Mensa had also got it right.

When I made it amply clear to Mom that we geniuses had no time at all to tidy up our rooms and keep them clean, and told bro in the same breath that we of the superior intellect do not share their aftershave lotions with mere humans, strangely enough, they did not seem thrilled. But it got Dad so cheesed off with me that he threatened to cut off my allowance.

Jeez! I don't think I will ever understand lesser mortals.

trouser belt—
the obese man tries to make
two ends meet

(Published in Prune Juice — March 2019 issue)

Checkmate

Ever since I read about Bobby Fischer's global fame and untold wealth I had always dreamt of playing chess at the World championship.

I could imagine myself ordering the organisers to arrange for pink spotlights. Not for the aesthetics but primarily because my complexion comes out beautifully on colour television. And of course, one wants to look one's best.

I would have dozens of frames made for my glasses to go with my extensive wardrobe of shirts. I spent sleepless nights deciding between a lemon-yellow shirt with a chocolate-brown tie and a pale-pink chemise with a maroon-coloured cravat. These things are of material importance to the Grandmaster. Insofar as shoes were concerned I found myself in a dilemma. Calf leather shoes looked swell but what of the brand? I vacillated between Jimmy Choo's and Todd's.

The suit had to be tailor-made in Savile Row, naturally. Complete with a matching pocket square. As for the cologne, I would settle for nothing less than the Paco Rabanne 'Million'. Even if it cost as much. After all, money was no problem at all while playing the Championship. Sponsors would pour it in by the buckets. Rather large buckets too. My mind made up I felt positively elated.

There remained only one minor point to be attended to. I still had to learn how to play the game.

Truckers' Union—
feeling quite awkward
in a tuxedo

(Published in Human/Kind Journal — February 2019 issue)

Cookbook for the Religious

How to Whip up a Delicious Omelette:

    Break one or two eggs — or three — into a steel container. You needn't be a glutton. Beat it to the rhythm of Michael Jackson's track Beat It, on the CD you bought last fall at the garage sale. Count your blessings. It isn't everyone who can boast of owning an iPod. Add salt and pepper to taste. Beat it again. Pour a little oil into the frying pan and heat gently over a slow fire. Pour the beaten eggs into the pan and pray. With your eyes closed. The almighty is watching. When you open your eyes if the omelette has been burnt to a crisp don't fret. All you need to do is pick up your cell phone and dial your favourite restaurant. Ever since free home delivery was invented there's been an answer to every such prayer. Having tackled the omelette issue think of what you would like to cook next.

    wrong number
    the chatty old lady
    undeterred

(Published in Haibun Today — March 2019 issue)

CROSSWORD EDITOR ORDERING A SIX-LETTER DRINK THAT STARTS WITH ω

Spellbound

I once knew a magician who owed me some money. A tidy sum. All his efforts to pull the moolah from his hat failed. That explained why he hadn't retired early. Faced with defeat he did a cowardly thing. Yes, he did the disappearing act. Without leaving a mailing address. But in the process I had learnt a few spells.

Goodness knows how but my little sister came to know about the sordid event. And threatened me with dire consequences if I didn't turn her into a ravishing beauty. Well, I figured there was no harm in trying.

I made her sit by the dining table and chanted the appropriate mantra. There was a puff of smoke and sis was transformed into an orange. I wasn't unduly bothered of course. Obviously, a syllable mispronounced. I pursed my lips and gave it another go. This time she became an egg. One of those hard-boiled varieties done over ten minutes. Now I was a trifle worried. I ransacked my memory and clearly enunciated the spell. I watched in despair as she turned into a bottle of Veuve Clicquot. Complete with ice bucket.

Not one to cry over spilt milk, or champagne, I poured myself a glass and relaxed as I thought it over. What with one thing and another, just as I swallowed the very last drop from the bottle Mother came along to ask me my sister's whereabouts. Of course, she didn't believe a word I said. She said I was drunk. Now a year has passed and Mom has given up all hopes. She presumes that sis must have eloped with the chauffeur. I can't argue with the logic.

The fact is that today I am one sister short.

    poll promises—
    another egg whizzes past
    the politico

(Published in Contemporary Haibun Online — April 2019 issue)

Putting on Dog

When my newly acquired friend, Mario, asked me over to his apartment for tea, I pulled on a rumpled T-shirt and distressed jeans and drove over.

It was with a jaunty step that I entered his pad and sank thankfully into a large armchair in his living room when my sensitive ears picked up a growl. One of those subdued growls that precede the lunge of a man-eating tiger. I looked at Mario with no little surprise. I mean, I knew he spoke several languages and dialects but this was new to me. And then my eyes travelled downward to a nasty looking canine who seemed to be all teeth.

Seeing my alarm Mario brushed aside the affair with a laugh. He assured me devil was just being amiable. Nevertheless, I eyed the critter with reservations as he continued slavering at the jaws and sharpening his fangs. Preliminary, no doubt, to sinking them into my neck and ripping out the jugular.

It was only when I flung cream crackers at him a few minutes later that the little beast accepted my friend request like a true Facebook fiend. And all along I had a feeling that he looked familiar. I could have sworn I had seen the little monster before. Then it struck me. He looked remarkably like my boss. Minus the horn-rimmed glasses and the handlebar moustache, of course. I was positive he shared a common lineage with my employer.

It is all in the genes I am told.

Kennel Club...
trying to trace the lineage
to Nehru's pet pooch

(A version of this appeared in Narrow Road — April 2019 issue)

Theory Weary

Dear Uncle Albert,

Your Theory of Relativity has really created waves and you are to be congratulated on that score. However, I have to indicate a few things that appear to have escaped your attention.

Mom is always finding fault with my lifestyle. She says I sleep all the time. When I pointed out to her what you have brilliantly derived—that time is relative, she pooh-poohed the idea. She refused to accept the fact that, for a certain inertial system, my nap of three hours could shrink to a mere three minutes and actually dismisses it as balderdash.

She also complains that I eat far too much — as if such a thing is possible! — and have become fat and lazy. Once again I showed her your clever equation that establishes mass-energy equivalence to point out to her that my extra bodyweight translates into lots and lots of energy. But all she could say was, I should have my head examined.

Uncle Al, you may have convinced the world of physicists that you are onto something hot, but unfortunately, you draw no dice whatsoever with your sister.

Your despairing nephew,
Otto

delusions—
the psychiatrist much concerned
with my bank balance

(Published in Human/Kind Journal — April 2019 issue)

Ship in a Bottle

A sailor friend once invited me for a cruise in the seas around the Gateway of India in south Mumbai. I was in the throes of indecision when he said that the motor launch in which we were to sail served beer and eats. That decided me. I accepted the invite. Fast as lightning. After all, the sea had always beckoned to me since I was so high.

We met at the pier where we were to board the boat. I stood on tiptoe and peered over shoulders to catch a glimpse of the beer bottles. I prayed fervently for my favourite brand. We sailors are a religious lot.

Finally the launch drew alongside and minutes later we were seated at a table for two with me drumming my fingers impatiently. Fifteen minutes later the vessel pulled away and I almost broke into a seaman's ditty.

I squinted into the distance and shouted, "Beer ahoy!" as a plump waiter hove into view laden with goodies.

My sailor friend pointed out the landmarks in the distance as our launch picked up speed. I nodded absently, for I was too busy sailing through the beer and the eats. Not to be put off, Popeye went on and on about Elephanta Caves now on the horizon. He waxed lyrical about the carvings of the god Shiva doing the Tandava while I kept the bearer dancing attendance to my whims. I mean, after all, a guy has got to eat. And drink too. No wonder Popeye was such a skinny runt. I supposed he survived on cans of spinach.

When I went home that evening I described the cruise in great detail to the folks. Beginning with the lager, the starters, the main course, and ending with the dessert.

No wonder so many youngsters in classics ran away to sea.

    con artist—
    a sculptor arrested chiselling
    his patron

(Published in Pins On A Map, The IN haiku Mumbai Anthology 2018)

Awash and Dry

When we had our washing machine delivered to our doorstep Mother behaved as though the god Shiva had himself lugged the machine over from his roosting grounds on Mount Kailash. Possible, I had to admit, but I thought rather poorly of gods taking on the form of grubby porters with their palms extended.

For the next few days Mom refused to use the machine. Preferring instead to get the clothes hand-washed by the maid. At least until the pundit came and told her the auspicious date on which to start.

Later in the day devotees from the neighbourhood came along with platters of flowers and coconuts, offerings for the new god. Boons were asked for and promises made. To the accompaniment of burning incense sticks and lighted oil lamps.

Finally the day dawned. The day on which the washer was to be first employed as prescribed by the Brahmin astrologer. But Mom was reluctant. She felt it would hurt the religious sentiments of the worshippers who had pinned their faith on her. Fancy using an incarnation of divinity for washing soiled underwear. She was shocked to the core at the suggestion.

The gizmo now stands in the drawing-room festooned with garlands of marigold and heavy with Vedic marks. A full-time priest squats before it chanting mantras to the accompaniment of tinkling bells while pilgrims devoutly circle the machine and make their offerings. All in all, a very religious atmosphere prevails with devotional songs being sung every evening and devotees milling around.

As to the small matter of our dirty linen, that problem has been solved as well. We get them washed and pressed at the laundry around the corner.

> temple till —
> the gambler drops an IOU
> onto the plate

(Unpublished piece)

Poetic Injustice

The other evening, being at a loose end, I decided to eat out. I drove over to Colaba Causeway and paced the pavements till I came across an eatery with the name, The Kebabs And What-Not Place. What particularly appealed to me was the promise of 'what-nots'. So, I entered the restaurant with a good deal of enthusiasm.

The burly Sikh at the door bowed so low he almost brushed my shoes. I was led to a table at the corner and made myself comfortable. A steward in a monkey suit of parrot green handed me the bill of fare.

A word about this menu card. It was not one of your run-of-the-mill affairs which state in very prosaic terms the dishes offered with the prices on the right-hand side at a respectable distance. This one was pure poetry. Every dish was described in words that would have made even Shakespeare come panting with his tongue lolling out. Consider the following for instance:

> Served on a bed of fragrant rice
> Our lentils curry, rich with spice

Now I have always been a lover of poetry. Ever since I had to memorise and recite, the boy stood on the burning deck... in the fifth grade with my arms behind my erect back. In fact, this poem on the card even beat the one on daffodils by William Wordsworth. I mean, whoever heard of eating daffodils.

All the dishes in the à la carte were likewise described, in meter and rhyme, and a short time later I had selected the ones I wanted to savour. I was practically singing as I waited for the order to materialise. True to form, the waiter came in bearing the tray aloft with a spring in his step. I was drooling as the good fellow served me the delicacies and could hardly wait to taste this sonnet of Indian cuisine. What can I say? One spoonful convinced me that the chef had a brighter future as a bard than as a cook. Suddenly the fare tasted like a badly written limerick. After suffering the agony of consuming the culinary disaster on my platter I made up my mind.

Yessir! I would give up poetry for good.

Western Cuisine...
the Maître d' decides it's high time
he learnt French

(Published in Failed Haiku — December 2019 Issue)

SNOWBOUND...
STILL TRYING TO GET OUTSIDE
THE SMELLY BLUE CHEESE

Pulling up Short

I had always prided myself as a math wizard. I had a way with numbers. I never could understand why Dad objected to my getting zero in the term exams. Ah! The romance and intrigue of the number zero! Ask any mathematician.

The numerologist at the street corner advised me that zero was my lucky number. So accordingly, while buying myself a lottery ticket for a prize of ten million rupees, after sifting through a thick pile, I zeroed in on one with the maximum number of zeroes. Of course, I was confident of winning. What bothered me was how to spend the swag.

Friends suggested that I invest the money wisely for my old age. I had a horse laugh. I felt that nothing could be more ridiculous. I had other plans. More pragmatic and realistic. I wondered whether to purchase a yacht or a private jet. Having always had my feet firmly planted on terra firma I decided on the yacht.

I imagined myself in a Hawaiian shirt and Bermuda shorts, a straw hat placed at a rakish angle atop my head, and a Cuban cigar clenched between my teeth. I strutted about on the deck cockily and was rudely brought back to the present when the lottery ticket vendor announced that the results of the draw had been declared. I was counting the currency notes already as I dashed forth to buy the printed results.

When I saw the results everything I'd heard about corruption in high places came flooding into my mind. Watergate and the Bofors scam f'rinstance. Why else would I not win a Paisa?

I had to thank my lucky stars I hadn't gone in for the Hawaiian shirt and the Bermudas.

newspaper headlines...
the pickpocket clicks his tongue
at the corruption

(Published in Cattails — October 2019 issue)

Strait and Narrow

I should have seen it coming. The writing was on the wall. I blame myself entirely for the lapse.

The fact was that my friend, Dinesh was a healthy youngster like the rest of us. He smoked pot, drank like a fish and flirted with anybody in skirts. He was also a lazy, good-for-nothing bum. You see what I mean. A perfectly normal young adult. The role model for other youth. And then it happened.

Dinu came to me the other day and confessed in a whisper that he had given up pot. For good. I was alarmed. He then landed a bombshell by admitting to having gone on the wagon. Yes. He would never, ever touch alcohol. I was shocked.

"Dinu," I pleaded. "You're cracking up. Come to your senses, old pal."

Then Dinesh went on to say that he would henceforth wear three-piece suits and attend to his father's business. No more dirty tees and torn jeans. To cap it all this included taking a bath every day. By then I was totally traumatised. I wept for him.

I have now taken an appointment with a psychiatrist for my unfortunate buddy. The shrink is quite confident that a few months of treatment should bring Dinu back to normal.

Meanwhile, I have been making the rounds of places of pilgrimage and offering prayers. Even breaking coconuts.

Benares...
no one recognises the priest
with his shirt on

(Published in Prune Juice — November 2019 issue)

Begging Your Pardon

The other day, when I placed a tenner in the outstretched palm of a beggar who stood below a footbridge, he sighed.

"It's the inflation," he said.

"Yes," I agreed, nodding sympathetically.

"A tenner is no longer what it used to be," he continued in the same vein. "Time was when a tenner was a fortune. Now it's an embarrassment."

This had me thinking. I almost gave him another tenner but wondered if that would be an added embarrassment.

"Life is so difficult these days," he said. "The wife cannot do without her kitty parties and the kids insist on 3-D television sets."

I shuffled my feet as I thought of my small television set in my small living room.

"The missus wears only designer saris with her diamond chokers," wept the mendicant. "And my teen sons like expensive jeans and exclusive footwear."

"Sorry for being outspoken, sir," I said. "But how come this choice of profession?"

He gave me a withering look.

"I was once a happy middle-class citizen myself," he said. "But when the wife and kids thrive on luxuries one has to move up the social ladder and into a penthouse. To keep up with the *Desais*. And the rents are exorbitant," he wailed.

I thanked my lucky stars I was still middle class.

shopping complex...
still trying to figure out
which way is up

(Published in Human/Kind Journal—Issue 1.8 and subsequently nominated for the Pushcart Prize)

Hard to Swallow

I got up this morning feeling very uneasy. I couldn't for the life of me make out what was wrong. When I mentioned this to my older brother he furrowed his brow.

"It could be hypertension," he said with a frown. I told him that that was under control. I was taking a pink and white tablet for my blood pressure.

After pondering on this for several moments he suggested that it could be an allergy. A reaction to something I ate, perhaps. I told him I was taking a small red pill for allergies.

"Ho!" he then exclaimed, rather like Santa Claus. "Then it's sure to be something to do with the liver." But I didn't drink, I pointed out to him. And nor did I smoke, I added, to pre-empt any diagnosis on his part regarding my lungs or throat or nose. But bro is a tough egg and not so easily beaten.

There was only one thing left, he said, in a voice of doom. I had to be suffering from bleeding duodenal ulcers. I was shocked. I knew it had to be something dreadful. I begged his pardon and asked him to spell out the words. Pretty silly it would look if I couldn't spell my ailment right.

Finally, full of trepidation, I visited the dispensary of our family physician. As he examined me, I waited for my worst fears to be confirmed. I even mopped the brow with my handkerchief from time to time. Then as I got off the examination table I looked fearfully at the good doctor.

"My dear fellow," he said solicitously. "Nothing to worry about. You are suffering from acute constipation, that's all. Be sure to take a spoonful of laxative before going to bed tonight."

Back home I nursed the severest doubts about the GP's diagnosis. Bro too was positive that mere constipation was not the answer. He was convinced that it had something to do with the gall bladder or pancreas. Possibly even the colon. I had to look them up in the *Concise Oxford Dictionary*.

I am now in the lengthy process of contacting a specialist. A highly qualified senior consultant. Maybe even a surgeon with an FRCS.

After all, it is always better to get a second opinion. Even if it's constipation.

medical camp...
the beggar quite worried
about obesity

(Published in Failed Haiku — September 2020 issue)

Hot Couture

When my friend, Dinesh, stoutly declared his intention of getting married, all his bachelor friends were aghast.

Of course, we thought he was pulling our legs. Some people have a bizarre sense of humour, you know. But his expression, that of a person placing the noose firmly around his own neck and testing the knot lest it fails, belied this assumption. Then we smelt his breath to see if he'd been having a few behind our backs. Here again, we were proved wrong. Finally, after every alternative avenue had been ruled out, we had to conclude his statement was true. Somebody suggested a therapist. Somebody else recommended a pilgrimage to Benares and the chanting of mantras. Eventually, however, we had to accept his decision as final. And that was that.

Now weddings, of course, are occasions when everyone dresses up as if for a masquerade ball. It goes without saying that if a guy was caught in graphic tees and torn jeans attending the binge, he would be politely told to use the service entrance. So, I visited an haute couture outlet that sold clothes suitable for festive occasions.

When I told the middle-aged saleslady what I was looking for she said, "Ah, I've just the thing for you."

She showed me a traditional Indian sherwani in beige with gold embroidery. When she was looking the other way, I sneaked a peek at the price tag. It said rupees one-hundred and fifty thousand. Stunned, I told her I found it unsuitable and asked to see something else. The next one was a pistachio-green bandhgala with silver and green motifs. Once again, the price tag, in six figures, scandalised me. I told the good lady that she was mistaken in assuming I was the bridegroom. I was only the unfortunate fellow's buddy, I said.

She said, "Oh, but the ones for the bridegroom are over here."

Curiosity got the better of me and I examined the price tags. They cost a whopping rupees two-hundred and fifty thousand and more. I almost fainted I think and the salesperson sprinkled some water on my face from a glass. Rose water.

Well, that decided me. I wrote my chum a brief note excusing myself from attending his marriage ceremony because, as I explained to him, my astrologer had warned me against it. Something to do with Saturn being at the wrong place at the wrong time. A flimsy reason no doubt but then I wasn't exactly Richard Branson or Anil Ambani. And the only suit I had of any value at all was my birthday suit.

nudist colony...
yet again the visitor asks
for the dress code

(Published in MacQueen's Quinterly— 2020)

The Moon and Tuppence

I just cannot comprehend why my girlfriend always complains about me. It's not as though I don't try to be witty, charming and social in my behaviour.

The other day when she suggested a candlelight dinner for two to set the mood I was gung-ho for it. Throughout the meal I entertained her with how nuclear-powered electricity differed from hydroelectric plant generated power. She kept rolling her eyes heavenward. Being myopic, I admit I accidentally jabbed her hand with my fork mistaking it for a sausage, but there really was no reason to make an infernal row. Such things happen all the time.

Afterwards, sitting on the park bench she pointed to the full moon with dreamy eyes. Of course, I took the hint. I am not the halfwit some people think I am. I told her in lurid detail all about the Apollo expeditions and the moon landing in 1969. Neil Armstrong, I told her earnestly, was a role model for the young. I wouldn't swear to it, of course, but she seemed distrait and disinterested. Perhaps she'd had too much to drink. I told her as much.

Later, when I dropped her home, she didn't even ask me inside. I'd kept the best part for the end. I had been raring to inform her about Quantum mechanics and, if time permitted, the String theory too. But she refused to entertain my invitation for a visit to the planetarium the next day and told me to go boil an egg. A request which confounded me because I prefer my eggs poached.

I don't think I will ever understand girls.

nightclub date...
wondering if a T-shirt and torn jeans
will do

(Published in Contemporary Haibun Online — October 2019 issue)

Upliftment

The famous philosopher J Krishnamurti often talked about visiting the spirit of the long-deceased Lord Maitreya and giving him an earful about what the politicians were up to now, and which film star was dating which film star and other such items of interest. I had always been sceptical about it. I mean, why would Lord Maitreya interest himself in Bollywood talk.

One day, lying down after a couple of beers, I felt lightheaded. Turning around, I found to my amazement, that I was outside my physical body and floating just above it. I was intrigued. The stuff they put in beer, I mean to say. I almost drafted a letter of complaint to the CEO of the brewery on the spot.

Drifting higher and higher I suddenly found myself in another dimension, another world. The ghosts of long-dead ancestors were tottering about and falling all over the place with bottles of scotch gripped in their paws. Some of them were hiccupping. Of course, I recognised the place. No wonder they call it the spirit world.

All of a sudden, my late grandpa hove into view. When I gave voice and waved cheerily at him he vanished and almost instantly materialised beside me.

"Sure beats walking!" said grandfather.

"You haven't changed a bit, Gramps," I said. "Grandma always called you lazy."

"*Sshhh...* for Christ's sake!" said the old man. "She's just around the corner. I don't want her to catch me with this..." he said, patting a flask in his hip pocket, with a wink.

"You always hated alcohol," I pointed out. "How come you changed your mind?"

"It's called enlightenment. When you suddenly realise the truth. That single malts are far, far superior to South Indian filter coffee," he said.

I think I rolled my eyes heavenward. Then all at once I blacked out and when I came to I was once again lying on the divan in the living room. With my feet on the cushions to the annoyance of my sister.

Later, when I related the incident to Mother, she was incredulous. Called the whole thing a wicked lie. Especially the bit about scotch being better than coffee.

I wouldn't know really. I have yet to get heady on a cappuccino.

crystal ball—
the gypsy seer reaches
for her glasses

(Published in Failed Haiku — August 2019 issue)

Weekly Horror-scope

Gemini:

Things could be stormy this week. Be particularly careful your wife doesn't catch you talking to your girlfriend on the cell phone. Wives are touchy about such things. Yes, it's ridiculous but there it is.

You will also come into a fortune in the next seven days. The fifty bucks your friend borrowed ages ago might be forthcoming. If you can persuade your buddy into coughing it up, that is. Just don't overdo the torture.

Expenses may be high this week. Your teenage daughter may finally succeed in her emotional blackmail and get you to buy her that iPhone X she has been hankering for. But for heaven's sake don't give her a free hand when she's shopping online. You might spend a lifetime paying off her dues.

Romance is in the air too. However, take it easy when meeting your neighbour's wife clandestinely. Especially if the said neighbour has a pitchfork handy while you're passing by. Fellows are unreasonably sensitive about their spouses' love lives. They hate to be excluded.

Apart from that, you have a great week to look forward to. Keep your chin up and head high. Even if you happen to be swathed in bandages. Which is a nice way to wrap up the week.

online store—
still weeping copiously
the shoplifter

(Published in Failed Haiku — July 2019 issue)

The Bitter Half

I have always been in favour of women's liberation and equal rights for ladies. Ever since I can remember. The way women were treated like slaves was enough to disgust a guy.

When I mentioned this to my spouse she stifled a yawn and said, "Yes dear."

I decided that it was high time the women of the house be made aware of the injustices they'd had to endure. For centuries. So, I herded together and informed the better half and my daughter how grossly unfair the system had been to them. Germaine Greer and Gloria Steinem had fought tooth and claw for the cause, I said through gritted teeth. Bra burning takes guts. I suggested they read The Female Eunuch for their edification.

Do you know, I asked them with a raised index finger, that women were not even allowed to vote. Now, I said, pontificating, females had not only the right to vote at every state-level poll they could also stand for election and participate in governing the nation. How about that! They were no longer mere sex objects to be used by men and discarded, I said grandly.

My wife and daughter both stretched and yawned in unison and my life partner handed me a broom while indicating the living room floor with a sweeping gesture.

"And after you're through dusting the house be so kind as to wash yesterday's dishes. They just keep piling up in the kitchen sink. Then there's the laundry to be done. There's a dear."

Now as I do the furniture in the drawing-room with an ache in the lower regions of the back and a crick in the neck which acts up every time I bend, I am filled with the deepest misgivings. Yes, I had touched upon freedom from slavery and women's suffrage, no doubt. I had objected severely to ladies being used as sex objects too, I thought grumpily. But whoever mentioned household chores!

women's forum...
all the menfolk discussing
the speaker's figure

(Published in World Haiku Review —August 2020 issue)

Ye Gods

A friend of mine has always been vociferous about the Hindu mystique. He has strong views on the concept of Hindutva and can tick off on his pinkies the various reasons for considering the faith in question superior to every other faith in the world.

The two of us had seated ourselves at a table in the Sri Krishna Bar when the conversation veered onto religion. It was when he was on his third single malt that he squinted fiercely and started quoting the Bhagavad Gita verbatim in the original Sanskrit. Without stumbling over a single syllable. I was amazed. I was positive he could recite Gunga Din backwards without a pause. I wasn't even confident enough to pronounce my own name and all I had was a bottle of lager. I was seriously entertaining the thought that maybe there was something to the practice of Hinduism after all.

After the fifth large malt, however, my friend revealed his fascist leanings by suggesting we split the tab.

    hands joined in prayer...
    wondering how to hold up
    my trousers

    (Published in Contemporary Haibun Online — July 2019 issue)

Tree is Company

There is a mango tree in our backyard. Upright and very proper in her demeanour. Well behaved too. At least she doesn't throw noisy parties and play loud music. Just the tree, in fact, to read my *haiku* out to. So, I gathered sheets of my poems, squatted under the boughs and read out my verse. All forty of them.

The mango tree listened patiently and attentively. Not a squeak out of her. I frowned as I remembered my childhood chum, Raju. A great buddy but very bad as an audience. Always interrupting. When I was through, the leaves rustled.

That evening, I cornered my sister in the living room and volunteered to read out my haiku to her. The session was a disaster. She kept yawning throughout and looking at the wall clock to see if it was time for dinner. I found it most disconcerting. I mentioned this to her. I told her in no uncertain terms that the mango tree in the yard was a far better listener than she.

I pointed out that, no doubt, the tree hadn't given three rousing cheers and applauded madly but at least I hadn't found her yawning and looking distracted.

Yes, indeed. There is much to be said in favour of trees. You can take it from me.

    digital watch
    ...still trying frantically
    to turn off the alarm

(Unpublished)

The Portraiture

When my older brother told me his friend was an artist who had won several national awards, naturally I was impressed. You have to be really very good to win the Padma Bhushan, you know. They don't exactly give them away. Being all thumbs myself, I couldn't draw anything other than a cheque on my bank. So, of course, I was enthused about meeting this painter bloke and asked bro when he could arrange his visit. I wanted to have my portrait painted by him, I informed bro. The older sibling was a little uncertain but promised to try. And that is how Mr Singh, the painter, happened to be at my home, eating plum cake and buttered toast with tea one evening.

> art show launched...
> a critic closely examines
> the samosas

While Singh laboured through the cake and toast, I was setting up his canvas and easel for him. Saved a lot of time. Finally, he got up from the dining table, burped and gently massaged his fingers prior to wielding the brush.

I sat on a footstool as rigidly as is possible while nursing an itch at the base of my spine that couldn't wait. When I wiggled my backside the artist bloke clicked his tongue and complained bitterly about uncooperative models and what he'd like to do to them. There was boiling oil involved in it if I remember rightly.

And finally, the portrait was done. Singh stepped back and squinted at the canvas. Apparently satisfied with his handiwork, he smiled broadly and grunted to me to come and look. I hopped to it. Like a rabbit on observing a crunchy carrot. I looked at the canvas closely for a long, long time. And my heart sank. Into the depths of my abdomen. I turned on the painter and demanded an explanation. After all, plum cake and buttered toast don't fall from heaven. Like manna. Neither does Darjeeling brew. To my consternation, Mr Singh took umbrage, packed up his belongings and left in a huff.

It was later that bro explained everything to me. He said he had known all along that a portrait was not a good idea. After all, he continued, Mr Singh was an abstract artist, don't you know?

I stared long and hard at the blotches of colour on the offending canvas that was supposed to be me.

gallery entrance...
the security guard shoos away
the artist

(Published in Failed Haiku — August 2020 issue)

Egg-ceptional

Bademiya's *baida roti** has to be eaten to be believed. What the roadside chef could do to an egg, would have made an egg roll over onto its back and kick its legs in the air in ecstasy. An egg ceased to be an egg. It became luxurious and otherworldly with a prominent halo around it.

Everybody who came to Colaba in South Mumbai made a beeline for Bademiya's. Royalty rubbed shoulders with cabbies and jostled with mendicants at this Mecca of epicures. The great equaliser, as some nerd once described it. And for once I would have patted the nerd on the back and beamed at him.

There was a bade miya making egg rolls here when I was a finger-licking boy of eight and there still was a bade miya making egg rolls here when I became a finger-licking man of sixty-four. Everything was the same except that I no longer shouted 'whoopee'. And that's because sis frowns on it. She says I should eat like a gentleman. Even if it's a gentleman with egg yolk smeared all over his face. But then she always has been conservative and orthodox in her views.

The stall being just behind the Taj Mahal Intercontinental, it was not unusual for gentlemen in three-piece suits to quaff single malts on the rocks at the Harbour Bar and then shamelessly nip out the backdoor to make pigs of themselves at Bademiya's.

Then the mogul expanded. From a small stall with a modest sign declaring he had no branches, he bought a room in the same alley, decorated and furnished it and distributed menu cards with raised prices.

I am told by reliable sources that the place has gone to seed. Egg rolls without the sour odour of sweat kneaded in just don't taste the same.

Harbour Bar...
the barkeep's disdainful sniff
at my orange juice

(CHO Editor's note. *Baida roti,* popular street food in Mumbai, is often translated as an egg roll. It is not to be confused with the Chinese egg roll, although the basic concept isn't too dissimilar. Bademiya is a chain of kebab shops and restaurants that was started by a man known as Bade Miya, sometimes transliterated as Bade Mia or Bade Miyan.)

(Published in Contemporary Haibun Online — 2018)

Issues with Paper Tissues

Our coffee shop group met again yesterday. As usual, we had great fun discussing a variety of earth-shaking matters. We deliberated and debated the discrepancies in cosmological models proposed in the present millennium, the plight of Rohingyas in Myanmar, malnutrition among children in Third World countries and whose turn it was now to go and order the cheeseburgers with fries. The last-named drew much concern from members who felt they would drop dead any moment due to starvation. One of them even commented that he knew precisely how the undernourished kids in Africa felt.

   Happy Hour—
   that sobering discovery

   you're a tenner short

(Published in Haibun Today — June 2019 issue)

Chasing the Sandman

My buddy Dinesh is a great guy but he has his shortcomings. Always shabbily dressed he tends to get distracted easily while being spoken to and his reading includes nothing more intellectually stimulating than comic books. Well, I took it upon myself to do something about the last mentioned. So, when he came over to my place next, I loaned him my copy of *Ulysses*. That's right. The classic by James Joyce.

Beholding the thick volume Dinu broke out in a sweat. He fingered it gingerly much as one would a venomous tarantula which one has grabbed mistaking it for a piece of cheese. I chuckled to impress upon him that it was going to be all right. Once you got started on it, it was a breeze, I told him. A real page-turner, yessir!

To stimulate an interest in it, I gave him a brief background of the book. The technique was called, stream of consciousness, I informed the poor sap who looked like a death row prisoner who has just spotted the hangman hurrying towards him.

"I know it looks intimidating," I said to Dinesh. "But afterwards you will be ever so grateful."

So Dinu clutched the volume to his bosom and made off for home.

A week later, when I answered the doorbell, he burst into my living room very excited.

"By golly, you were right!" he said, clapping me repeatedly on the back until my vertebral column looked like it was turning to jelly. I had to hold him at arm's length before he could do any serious damage.

"Did you read it?" I asked my childhood chum.

"Of course, I did," he said, beaming. "I had barely read three pages before I fell into a deep, deep sleep. And you know I always suffered from insomnia."

Now he refuses to return the book.

Juhu Beach...
still patting the earth flat
after the camel ride

(Published in the QuillS—December 2020 issue)

MOULIN ROUGE —
TORN BETWEEN BOEUF BOURGUIGNON
AND SAMOSAS

Turning on the Juice

When my friend, Dinesh, invited me over to his place for drinks on his sixtieth birthday I was in two minds. Of course, I wanted to wish him on this special occasion, but I had strong reservations about drinking alcoholic beverages. So, I sent him a politely worded message declining the invite. Pat came his reply that he knew all about my abstinence and he had therefore arranged soft drinks for me. Well, put that way, how could I refuse. So, on the appointed day at the appointed time I rang the doorbell at the entrance to the palatial mansion that he called home and was met at the door by Dinesh himself, all wreathed in smiles.

Some of his other guests had already arrived and were apparently into their second or third drink, judging from the banter and the raised tones. Dinu led me to the makeshift bar and I ordered a glass of chilled orange juice. Pretty soon I was parking my butt on a soft yielding settee and making myself comfortable.

The orange juice was delicious, the company congenial and the ambience luxurious. It was when I was on my third orange juice and explaining to a novice the intricacies of the stock market and how to make a killing that I noticed my friend's facial features blurring. When I mentioned this the friend suggested a good ophthalmologist and even recommended some eye drops. Another thing I noticed, was an irresistible urge on my part to burst into laughter and slap my thighs. Even when nobody was joking. I felt so much at home in these surroundings that I soon raised my feet and tucked them beneath me on the settee. Which turned out all right because many of the others had removed their jackets and loosened their neckties.

    playing the market
    …still worried sick over
    how to spend a billion

It was only when Dinu shook me awake and told me it was time to go home that I came back to earth. Waving goodbye to everybody, I asked the good barkeep what type of juice he had been serving me. He said it was canned orange juice imported from sunny California, no less. It always goes so well with the vodka, he added brightly.

new contact lenses...
my nephew says I look funny
without glasses

(Published in Failed Haiku — February 2021 issue

Salt and Pepper

When my brother and I went boating on the lake at Mahabaleshwar, we were confident that we could handle the boat and the situation. As the lady at the office there asked us whether we knew boating, we almost laughed in her face. Fancy asking two seasoned salts like us the question. We could barely contain our mirth. So off we went and selected a small boat with paddles and paddle-locks or whatever they are called. The boat was pushed ahead into deeper waters by the fellow on the bank and we were adrift. We both sat at opposite ends of the same seat and heaved at the paddles. Oddly enough, the vessel started rotating about an axis and tracing circles. Then we realised our boo-boo. Bro and I were past masters at paddling, but we happened to be doing it in opposite directions.

Suddenly the grey-haired lady at the boat office onshore started shouting through a megaphone. We almost dismissed her as excitable till we realised we were on a collision course with another boat which was being steered by two inept steerers. They narrowly missed us and then my paddle fell overboard. Since a boat cannot be driven with a single paddle we started hollering for the coastguard. After a few minutes, an employee of the office rowed alongside, hopped aboard and took us safely ashore. Even for two old salts like us the voyage had been much too exciting and we collectively heaved a giant sigh of relief.

Over dinner that night we both agreed that they just didn't make boats like they used to any more.

> hill station
> still trying to get over
> the vertigo

(Published in Pins On A Map, The IN haiku Mumbai Anthology 2018)

Concluded...